Groton Monument Assoc.

Celebration of the One Hundred and Tenth Anniversary of the Battle of Groton Heights

Groton Monument Assoc.

Celebration of the One Hundred and Tenth Anniversary of the Battle of Groton Heights

ISBN/EAN: 9783337390259

Printed in Europe, USA, Canada, Australia, Japan

Cover: Foto ©Andreas Hilbeck / pixelio.de

More available books at **www.hansebooks.com**

Groton Monument Association.

CELEBRATION
OF THE ONE HUNDRED AND TENTH ANNIVERSARY OF THE BATTLE OF GROTON HEIGHTS.

FIRST DECENNIAL COMMEMORATION: SECOND CENTURY.

NEW LONDON, CONN.

MORNING TELEGRAPH PRESS.

1891.

OFFICERS OF THE ASSOCIATION.

PRESIDENT.
ERASMUS D. AVERY.

VICE PRESIDENTS.

FREDERICK BILL,	WILLIAM H. ALLEN,
THOMAS A. MINER,	NELSON H. BURROWS,
THOMAS F. MORGAN,	LORENZO D. BAKER,
HENRY BILL,	ELISHA A. HEWITT,
JOHN T. WAIT,	IDA S. BAKER,
ROBERT A. GRAY,	CLARA B. WHITMAN,

HENRY LARRABEE.

SECRETARY, *pro tem*, AND TREASURER.
PHILO LITTLE.

EXECUTIVE COMMITTEE.
BENJAMIN STARK, Chairman.

FREDERICK BILL,	LORENZO D. BAKER,
CHRISTOPHER L. AVERY,	NATHAN S. FISH.

Prefatory Note.

The Battle of Groton Heights, fought September 6, 1781, on a commanding hill upon the left or eastern bank of the Thames River, opposite the town of New London (which at that hour was wrapped in flames from Arnold's torches) was a memorable and momentous action, second only to Bunker Hill, perhaps, in its decisive consequences.

Its immediate result, like that of Bunker Hill, was defeat for the patriots upon the actual field. Yet, as the defeat suffered by Putnam and Prescott, on those Charleston heights across the water from Boston, was accounted a virtual victory in its effect upon the British troops and the ensuing campaign, so the reverse endured by Colonel Ledyard on Groton Heights—with the sacrifice of his own life and the lives of so many among his intrepid, unconquerable followers—became practically a triumph over the enemy. It stopped Benedict Arnold's inroad upon Connecticut, led to his withdrawal, and foiled Clinton's plans.

Thus the gallant opposition of the Americans at Bunker's (or Breed's) Hill, ending with retreat, in the beginning of the Revolution, was fitly supplemented by their fellow American volunteers of Connecticut, toward the end of the war, in that brave stand made within Fort Griswold at Groton, which ended in devoted massacre. The scenes of these two battles form harmonious pendants in the broad gallery of thought wherein our national memory cherishes pictures of the martial and self-sacrificing deeds done by our sires.

In course of time the anniversary of this heroic struggle

came to be observed with patriotic and commemorative ceremonies every year. On one of these occasions, in 1879, the
Groton Monument Association, which had received custodian-
ship of the granite shaft erected in honor of the martyrs, near
the old fort, appointed a committee to "make arrangements
for the One Hundredth Anniversary" of the battle; namely,
in 1881. An account of the work done by this committee,
and by the large number of ladies and gentlemen who were
called to aid it, may be found in the substantial and interesting volume on the Battle of Groton Heights compiled by
William W. Harris, revised, enlarged with notes and published
by Charles Allyn (New London, 1882). That work, also,
chronicles the superb success which crowned the labors of the
Centennial Committee. Liberal sums were appropriated for
their use, by Congress and the Legislature of Connecticut; a
number of United States war-ships assisted in the celebration;
and the National Guard of Connecticut took part with veterans
of the Union Army, in a brilliant and realistic sham fight
which reproduced the manœuvres of the Americans and
British with historical accuracy. Many thousands of citizens
gathered from all quarters to watch this imposing spectacle,
and to listen to the oration, poems and addresses which were
delivered in a great tent spread on the hill-top.

Believing with George Bancroft that the courage and love
of country shown by Ledyard and his comrades "should be
celebrated not only at the end of a century, but of a thousand
years," yet realizing, perhaps, that enthusiasm, like powder,
should be stored for use at the most effective moment—the
Monument Association wisely resolved, in the year of this
great celebration, that the day should be commemorated hereafter, *not* annually, but once in ten years.

The first decennial celebration, therefore, took place in 1891.

The writer of this Prefatory Note, having been asked to arrange for publication the records of the First Decennial Celebration in the Second Century, submits them herewith to those whose patriotism, sincere though undemonstrative, may prompt them to keep such mementoes and to continue, in coming times, the tribute due to our Revolutionary heroes.

GEORGE PARSONS LATHROP.

NEW LONDON, October, 1891.

FIRST DECENNIAL COMMEMORATION

In the Second Century since the Battle of Groton Heights.

[One Hundred and Tenth Anniversary, Celebrated Sept. 8, 1891.]

In 1889, a Special Committee of the Groton Monument Association was appointed to report at the next Annual Meeting "a plan for a suitable commemoration of the Battle of Groton Heights, on the 6th of September, 1891."

In 1890 the Special Committee, thus empowered, made by its chairman, Benjamin Stark, the following report:

"Resolved, that the Groton Monument Association, incorporated by the Commonwealth of Connecticut, and charged with the care and preservation of the Monument erected by the State on Groton Heights in memory of the noble men who were killed in Fort Griswold on the 6th of September, 1781—and by all appropriate means to perpetuate the memory of their heroic sacrifices—will, at the next annual meeting of the Association, on the 6th of September, 1891, commemorate with public exercises the *First Decennial Anniversary in the Second Century* of that immortal day in the annals of Connecticut; a day of such momentous consequences in the struggle of the United Colonies for Liberty and Independence.

"Resolved, that Benjamin Stark, John T. Wait and Nathan S. Fish be and they are hereby appointed a Committee to prepare and present to the next General Assembly of the State a memorial requesting said General Assembly to appropriate $——— to aid in defraying the expenses incurred by the Association in the commemoration of said First Decennial Anniversary, and to invite the Governor, escorted by the Governor's Guards, to be present on said day and review such portion of the State National Guard as may deem it expedient to assemble under arms, to participate in the services of the day."

Benj: Stark

" Resolved, that Christopher L. Avery, Frederic Bill, Nathan S. Fish and E. A. Hewitt of the town of Groton ; George F. Tinker, William Belcher, Philip C. Dunford and Walter Learned of the town of New London ; John T.Wait, Solomon Lucas, Henry Bill and Gardiner Greene, Jr., of the town of Norwich; Richard A. Wheeler and Ephraim Williams of the town of Stonington; John Brewster of the town of Ledyard ; James Allyn of the town of Waterford ; and Charles S. Johnson of the town of Montville be and they are hereby invited and authorized in behalf of the Association to act as a General Committee to carry out the purposes set forth in the foregoing Resolutions.

"'And that the President of the Association, Erasmus D. Avery, be made and he is hereby appointed Chairman of said Committee.

" And as said public exercises in commemoration of said Anniversary are, in contemplation of said resolution, to occur hereafter but once in ten years, that said Committee be requested to make this Decennial Commemoration, to the best of their ability and the pecuniary means placed at their disposal, worthy of its patriotic and hallowed associations."

The report was adopted; and the General Committee was authorized to fill any vacancies that might occur in said Committee by death, resignation or declination to serve thereon, and in its discretion, by a majority of all the members thereof, from time to time, to add to its numbers.

In 1891, on the 22d of July, the General Committee met in the Council Chamber of the City Hall in the City of New London, and organized by the appointment of Benjamin Stark as Chairman of the Committee, in place of Erasmus D. Avery, who by reason of his age and infirmity declined to serve. Philo Little of Groton was elected Secretary of the Committee.

Walter Learned, George F. Tinker and Solomon Lucas were appointed a committee on Literary Exercises.

On the 22d of July, pursuant to adjournment, the committee met and completed its organization by the appointment of the following committees :

On Invitation and Reception.

Walter Learned, N. S. Fish, James Allyn, Richard A. Wheeler and Charles S. Johnson.

On Finance.

Frederic Bill, William Belcher and Gardiner Greene, Jr.

On Grounds.

Nathan S. Fish, E. A. Hewitt and Ephraim Williams.

On Transportation.

Philip C. Dunford, John Brewster and E. A. Hewitt.

Again, on the 26th of August, the committee met, pursuant to adjournment. It then received and adopted the reports of the several committes, and approved the final arrangements planned for the public exercises, as embodied in an " Order of Exercises" prepared by the chairman of the general committee.

Unfortunately, the disputed election of 1890, for Governor and other executive officers of the commonwealth, and the " deadlock" which ensued between the Senate and the House of Representatives of the Connecticut Legislature of 1891, made it impossible to apply for that appropriation from the State, which the general committee had originally hoped to obtain. The funds needed for carrying out a proper observance of the day were, therefore, raised by contribution from a small number of friends of the cause. The amount of money at the disposal of the committee was inevitably somewhat limited, notwithstanding the cordial and generous co-operation of these friends. But, as the event proved, their support was rewarded by a dignified, picturesque and enthusiastic celebration, of the sort which it so well deserved.

The commandant of Fort Trumbull, also, by lending a company of regulars of the United States Artillery, and the senior officer of the North Atlantic Squadron anchored in the harbor—who sent ashore a company of marines and three hundred blue jackets equipped as infantry, to take part in the ceremonies and parade—added to the occasion, through their courtesy, its finest element of display.

The 6th of September falling, this year, on Sunday, it was resolved by the committee to hold the appointed exercises on the following day. In consequence of heavy rain on Monday, however, the proceedings were postponed until the next morning. Owing to this unavoidable change, the New London battalion of the National Guard, which was to have paraded on Monday (a legal holiday), could not be mustered to join in the celebration.

The exercises occurred at 11 A. M. on Tuesday, September 8th, according to the programme which is printed below:

ORDER OF EXERCISES.

Dirge, Third Regiment Band, C. N. G.

Invocation, Rev. N. T. Allen, Chaplain Third Regiment, C. N. G.

National Air, Third Regiment Band, C. N. G.

Address, Rev. A. J. McLeod, Pastor Groton Congregational Church.

National Air, Third Regiment Band, C. N. G.

Poem, Mrs. Rose Hawthorne Lathrop, read by George Parsons Lathrop, Esq.

Anthem—America, led by Groton Choir.

1 My country! 'tis of thee,
Sweet land of liberty,
   Of thee we sing:
Land where my fathers died!
Land of the Pilgrims' pride!
From every mountain side
   Let freedom ring!

2 My native country, thee—
Land of the noble free—
   Thy name—I love;
I love thy rocks and rills,
Thy woods and templed hills;
My heart with rapture thrills
   Like that above.

3 Let music swell the breeze,
And ring from all the trees
   Sweet freedom's song:
Let mortal tongues awake;
Let all that breathe partake;
Let rocks their silence break,—
   The sound prolong.

4 Our fathers' God ! to thee,
   Author of liberty,
     To thee we sing:
   Long may our land be bright
   With freedom's holy light ;
   Protect us by thy might,
     Great God, our King!

Auld Lang Syne, Third Regiment Band, C. N. G.

Benediction, Rev. Wm. L. Peck, Episcopal Church, Groton.

The subjoined description of the events of the day is reprinted from the New London *Morning Telegraph* of Wednesday, September 9, 1891 :

THE ONE HUNDRED AND TENTH ANNIVERSARY OF THE GROTON MASSACRE.

A more agreeable day than dawned on the public yesterday could not have been desired for the Groton commemorative exercises. Had Monday been as well favored by nature, there would have been a thousand people where there were a hundred yesterday, and the military display would have been of a more imposing character. But as it was, the projectors of the exer-cises have no reason to complain. The programme was carried out on the first lines, and everything passed off most happily and most successfully. The attendance was larger than was expected for a working day, and many came a great distance to be present at the exercises. It was, of course, Groton's day, and the population of the town were out doors where they could best witness what was going on. Aside from the exercises there was the novelty of seeing several companies of blue-jackets in line— a rare spectacle even in this seaport town of naval distinction.

The military bodies participating were the battery from Fort Trumbull, under command of Lieut. Catlin, a company of marines from the U. S. S. Philadelphia, and five companies of blue-jackets from the three warships, the Philadelphia, Petrel and Enterprise, all under command of Lieut. J. C. Fremont, of the Philadelphia ; the officers of the New London Naval Station ; veterans of W. W. Perkins Post, Col. W. H. Bentley in command ; and members of the Loyal Legion, O. U. A. M., George W. Randall, captain. Could the celebration have taken place Monday, to this military contingent would have been added the companies of the local battalion of the Third Regiment, C. N. G., and uniformed civic societies. The music was by the Third Regiment band, E. A. Colby, leader, and the Marine band of the Philadelphia, G. Savasta, leader.

Col. George Haven, of the Third, was chief marshal, with Lieut. W. E. Pendleton as aid.

The marines and blue-jackets landed in Groton from their large barge in tow of launches, and the military from this side of the river crossed on the 10.30 trip of the Uncas. Immediately on arrival in Groton the line for parade was formed on Thames street in the following order :

Third Regiment Band; Battery L, Second Artillery, Fort Trumbull; Band of U. S. S. Philadelphia; Company of Marines; Three Hundred Blue-jackets; Perkins Post, G. A. R.; Fort Griswold Commandery, L. L., O. U. A. M. : Hon. Benjamin Stark, chairman executive committee, Rev. A. J. McLeod, orator of the day; Commodore Fyffe and Paymaster Martin of the New London Naval Station, Commander Pigman, Lieut. McKenzie and naval staff in carriages.

The route was down Thames to Broad, up Broad to Monument, to the fort. The preparation for the exercises within the fort consisted of the erection of a canvas-covered, flag-draped platform and the placing of seats in front of the audience. A large number of spectators had already secured seats of advantage from which to witness the exercises.

On the platform were seated Benjamin Stark, the chairman of the executive committee, who was to preside over the exercises ; Rev. A. J. McLeod, who was to deliver the oration; George Parsons Lathrop and Mrs. Lathrop, the former to read the poem written by Mrs. Lathrop; Rev. N. T. Allen, who was to deliver the invocation ; Rev. William L. Peck, who was to give expression to the benediction at the close of the exercises ; Frederick Bill, the president of the association, who was elected the day previous to succeed E. D. Avery, resigned on account of ill health ; Judge Richard A. Wheeler, of Stonington, who was president of the association ten years ago when the centenary celebration was held; R. A. Gray, who succeeded Mr. Wheeler as president; Mayor George F. Tinker of New London; Deacon Chester, a native of and former resident of Groton, now residing in Washington; Asa Lathrop, 2d, Jonathan Trumbull, of Norwich; Elisha H. Palmer of Montville, Nathan S. Fish, Philo Little, Commodore Fyffe and other naval officers, and several ladies.

In front and facing the platform were several rows of seats placed there for the benefit of the audience. On the sloping sides of the fort, hundreds, either standing or seated, were in convenient distance to observe all that was done and hear all that was said.

When the exercises were about to open after the arrival of the military, the scene presented inside the fort was one that would interest any spectator. Drawn up in line at the rear of the seats and facing the platform were the regulars from Fort Trumbull. At their right was the Third Regiment band. Back of the regulars was the company of marines from the U. S. S. Philadelphia and the Marine band; behind were the five companies of blue-jackets, and on all sides were the spectators. It was a scene that an artist would have delighted to portray.

THE EXERCISES AT THE FORT.

The exercises began a few minutes after 11 o'clock with a dirge by the Third Regiment band, and when the music had ceased Mr. Stark advanced to the front of the platform and said: "On behalf of the Groton Monument Association, and in the absence of the president, the pleasant duty devolves upon me as chairman of the executive committee, to extend a most cordial welcome to those assembled to-day to do honor to the brave men who laid down their lives on this hallowed spot in defense of the liberties of America. They put their trust in God and though slain they were not confounded. Their successors to the latest generation, who shall enjoy the liberties which they helped to achieve, may and ought to exclaim, ' We will magnify Thee, oh Lord, and exalt Thy name forever, for the great things which

Andrew James McLeod

Thou didst for our fathers in their day and generation.' It was appropriate on this solemn occasion that the ceremonies should begin by invoking His holy name. Rev. N. T. Allen, chaplain of the Third regiment, commenced the exercises by reading a portion of holy scripture and invoke the divine blessing."

The veteran chaplain of the Third then advanced to the edge of the platform, and asked that God might with kindliness look upon the people here assembled. He read Scripture extracts that were appropriate to the commemorative exercises, and then gave way to Mr. Stark, who introduced Rev. A. J. McLeod, the pastor of the Groton Congregational church, to whom fell the duty of delivering the address.

In the course of Mr. Stark's introduction he said : " There were eighty-five victims on that deplorable day, and of this number sixty men and boys were from the town of Groton, most of whom were members of the Groton Congregational church. It is a felicitous circumstance on this occasion that the address will be delivered by the present pastor of the ancient church, whom I now introduce."

Rev. Mr. McLeod then read from manuscript his well-prepared and most interesting address.

ORATION DELIVERED BY REV. A. J. McLEOD,

Mr. President and Fellow Citizens :

I am pleased to meet an assembly like this on this Decennial day, convened for the purpose of keeping fresh in the memory one of the most remarkable events in our nation's history. The day belongs not to a local issue, to a partial interest however sacred that issue or interest may be in itself. The day, the event, is national, and should be so considered, and when celebrated so celebrated. The battle of Groton Heights commemorates one of the most important events in our revolutionary struggle, allied as it is so closely with Yorktown. But why, it may be asked, commemorate these acts of more than a hundred years ago. I answer, for this reason : Our revolutionary struggle not only marks the birth of this now mighty nation, but it also marks an era in the ascendancy of the intellectual over the physical in man. It marks the period when no longer the tallest, but the wisest should govern. Our ancestors were never vassals, they were English gentlemen, occupying high social positions, persons of wealth and intelligence; they were the men who stood with the foremost men of every nation; and we must not look upon them as some of the English looked upon them in the days of the Revolutionary War, and now would if they dare, as felons banished from their country, but we must look upon them as English gentlemen. Had England been wise and allowed Patrick Henry, or George Washington, or any of that noble galaxy of men whose names are a household word, as they are enrolled on that inspiring document, the Declaration of Independence, to represent the colonies in the parliament of Great Britain, there would have been no revolution, and these states to-day would have been the richest possession of the English crown. But our fathers were men of renown and determination who fully appreciated their rights; for which they declared, for themselves and their posterity, that where there is no represention there shall be no taxation. Denied represcntation, they withheld taxation; they asserted the rights of freemen; they announced the ultimate principles of human rights, and thus inaugurated the grandest political era in the annals of time.

The main interest of American history has naturally enough accumulated around the crisis which formally divorced us from the mother land. In the contemplation of this period our attention is often diverted from the true date and origin of American liberty. The Declaration of 1776 asserted our independence, but did not by any means create it; neither the sentiment in the minds of the states nor the reality in their institutions.

Both the sentiments and the institutions of the country were as essentially democratic two hundred years ago as they are to-day. They were the natural outgrowth of the soil. Other sentiments or institutions unfriendly to liberty could never gain foothold on these shores.

In the first organization of their legislative assemblies, the prophetic sense of the colonists resisted the encroachments of their rulers. For, said they, "the waves of the sea do not more certainly waste the shore, than the minds of ambitious men are led to invade the liberties of their brethren." And in justice to them and in the spirit of their comparison, we may say that the stern and rock-bound coast does not more surely repel the advancing surge than the stern and sturdy souls of the Pilgrims repelled the advances of civil usurpation. The causes which led to our separation would hardly have been deemed sufficient had not the people been ripe for independence. The stamp act, which the stern resistance of our fathers forced the British government to repeal before it could fairly take effect, however odious in its principle, was not so threatening in its consequences that the citizens of Boston should have ushered it in with the ringing of bells and funeral orations to departed liberty. The addition of three pence a pound on tea could hardly be considered a national calamity. The nation would have pocketed the injustice indemnifying themselves as best they might. But they had breathed the air of freedom for over a century and a half, and they did not propose to submit to any English oppression. They were already independent; they always had been so, ever since Smith and Carver, and Winthrop and Williams had labored. It was for the sake of this independence they had braved the perils of the deep and the greater perils of the wilderness. With a great sum they had obtained this freedom and they had no intention of selling it cheaply. They were already independent; they always had been. God willing, they always meant to be; and when the decisive moment came they had nothing to do but to declare their intention.

I now turn from the causes which led to the great act, to the act itself, and to-day it is only necessary for me to call your attention to a few leading facts, knowing as I do the history of the revolutionary struggle is familiar to you all. Passing then, as I do, much that is national, I come to that which belongs to us as a state, as a community. The Connecticut authorities had been indefatigable in raising and provisioning troops, and her people had been equally earnest in offering their services from the beginning. In the number of the men contributed she stood second of the states, with her 31,936 men, Massachusetts being first with her 67,907. Many of these men have left their names enrolled in the history of fame. There is Jonathan Trumbull, the revolutionary governor, known in history as "Brother Jonathan," Israel Putnam, "who dared to lead where any dared to follow," Huntington of Norwich, Terry of Enfield, and others almost too numerous to mention. Washington spoke of the Connecticut brigade "as composed of as fine a body of men as any in the army." In almost all cases Connecticut men were drafted into service outside of the state to make good the deficiency of less zealous states.

New London and vicinity had long been regarded by the British with especial enmity. The people of this vicinity were intensely patriotic. Large quantities of supplies were stored here, and its beautiful harbor, which is our pride and glory, afforded a safe refuge for the largest ships. Privateers were here fitted out, which showed the greatest bravery and accomplished grand results. It was a time when about every community had to maintain the defence of its own border, and in order to do this she must rid herself of her foes within. Consequently the crown Tories were driven to Long Island, while the Long Island Whigs crossed into Connecticut, and so the waters of the Sound were harassed by almost continual skirmishing. When the French forces were quartered within the state her people enjoyed a season of comparative tranquility. When they were withdrawn for the march on Yorktown, which had been planned by General Washington and the French leaders, the state was left as usual, almost unsupported.

Let me for a moment call your attention to the relation of the British and American armies at this time. The enemy was transferring the war to the south. Their plan was to begin south and conquer northward. Then in case they were forced to make peace, they hoped to be able to keep the southern territory, believing that a part would be better than none; and about the first of August, Cornwallis went to Yorktown intending to permanently establish himself; and so confident was he that he could hold his position that on the 22nd of August he wrote Sir Henry Clinton at New

York, offering to send him 1,000 or 1,200 men to assist against the allied forces (Americans and French) under Washington.

It was just at this critical juncture that Washington received the glorious news that Count DeGrasse had left St. Domingo with twenty-five or thirty ships, and his first landing would be on the shores of the Chesapeake. Washington immediately sent a messenger to Lafayette informing him of this, and telling him to stop by all means any effort on the part of Cornwallis from retreating into North Carolina. It was also at this time, and there seems to be no reason for it, Cornwallis assisted in this very movement by concentrating all his forces in the immediate vicinity of Yorktown; so that the French commanders on shipboard could watch his every movement. Washington now, to keep Clinton alarmed for the safety of New York, concentrated his forces up the Hudson, which led to the belief he was to move immediately on that city, but instead of this he starts secretly for Virginia, that he may capture Cornwallis and his army.

The movements of the American army at this time are exceedingly rapid. Passing through Jersey the army reaches the Delaware before Clinton had time to think of what he was doing. As soon as Clinton realized Washington's movements he called a council of his generals, and they unanimously concurred that the only thing for them to do was to go to the succor of Cornwallis. And here is a difficult question to settle. Was it Clinton's intention to reach Virginia by way of New London, or did he purpose checking any re-enforcements from New England. One thing is certain; and that is it had been the intention of Tryon's expedition, in 1779, against New Haven, Fairfield and Norwalk, to include New London. But Wayne's capture of Stony Point changed the basis of action. Another thing is true; and that is, by the Tories this vicinity was hated. It was rightly regarded a dangerous place. It contained at that moment a great store of supplies. The ship Hannah had just been brought into port, a prize worth $400,000. Doubtless all of these things combined, and the fact also Benedict Arnold (whose name I disdain mentioning, as the bare mention of the name gives it a prominence which it should never have unless it be in contempt) was idle and impatient. He, a native of Norwich, knew the country around New London well, and its defenceless condition was no secret to him. Two forts had been thrown up, Fort Trumbull, and Fort Griswold in which we are at this time assembled. The former, Fort Trumbull, was open at the rear and had a garrison of but twenty-three men, who were ordered to retreat to Groton, or Fort Griswold, at the approach of danger. Colonel William Ledyard was in command of both forts. Arnold's landing on the 6th of September seems to have been a surprise. True, the people had been informed that late the night before a large fleet had been seen sailing close under Long Island shore; but many a fleet had sailed the Sound during the war and passed New London, and so, thinking no harm was nigh, they retired as usual. Day dawned, and what was the astonishment of the people to see eight war ships ready to enter the harbor. The signal was given which was to call the people to arms, but a Tory had given Arnold the signal, and so he was enabled to counteract it. Ledyard sent messengers into the country to carry the alarm, and knowing the character of the people we are justified in saying, that as Paul Revere on his foaming horse rode on the 19th of April, 1775, so rode those brave men on September 6th, 1781. For Colonel Ledyard hoped that the people from the country would arrive in season to help him defend this fort, as he had resolved, come what would, to hold it. If this be not true I fail to see the force of those immortal words of his, "If I must to-day lose honor or life, you who know me well can tell which it will be." Fort Trumbull was taken with a rush. The twenty-three men under Captain Shapley had only time to fire one round, spike their guns, leap into their boats, and start for this fort, where Colonel Ledyard was in command. Arnold hastened on to the town and began his congenial work of burning and plundering. On this side of the river, at the same time, a brave fight was going on. Fort Griswold was a much stronger fort than Trumbull. Its walls were then ten feet high, with a deep ditch outside, and there were within one hundred and fifty men, most of them farmers and citizens of the patriotic town, who had seized their guns and hastened to defend the fort when they heard the booming of the cannon. Colonel Eyre had landed at Eastern Point with eight hundred men, about the same time Colonel Robinson landed with his men on the New London side. These men, by ledges used as a shelter, had gotten within a few hundred feet of the fort. It is now "high twelve," and Colonel Eyre sends a white flag toward the fort demanding unconditional surrender. Colonel Ledyard summons his officers, Captains Avery, Stanton and Williams. Defend the fort they say ; and the officer goes back with this message, only to return with another that, "unless you surrender no quarter will be given." Captain Shapley has now reached the fort with his few who had survived the British attack, and so Colonel Ledyard sends out the reply of the brave men : "We shall not surrender let the consequences be what they may." Colonel Eyre prepares to advance. He will, as the commander who has just taken Fort Trumbull, make a rush, leap the ditch; climb the wall and get inside the fort before they can reload, after their firing once. But he knew not his men. Captain Halsey is standing by an eighteen pounder. He is an old sailor and been in many a fight. He rams home two bags full of grape shot. The British move toward the fort. The captain runs his eye along the cannon ; they are in range. Bang! goes the cannon, the air is filled with shot and twenty men go down. From every available spot fire goes forth. The ground is strewed with killed and wounded. Major Montgomery now commands, and his men rush into the ditch ; they are so near the cannon cannot harm them. In order now to enter the fort they must tear away the pickets, which run out from the walls over the ditch. Major Montgomery, a brave officer, attempts to climb the pickets and falls mortally wounded into the ditch upon the heads of his men. But it is a battle of seven to one. Soon British soldiers are seen leaping from the parapet, unbowing the gate and rushing in. Col. Eyre and Major Montgomery having fallen, Major Bromfield commands ; and so, upon entering the fort, shouts, "Who commands here ? " "I did, but you do now," is Ledyard's reply, handing him his sword. Bromfield, infuriated by the unexpected slaughter, plunges it to the hilt into Ledyard's breast. With such an example from one in authority, the soldiers' instincts came out at their worst. I say instinct (for a British soldier is only an animal), the defenders were bayoneted wherever they sought refuge, until all but about twenty-five of the one hundred and fifty were killed or desperately wounded. For the credit of humanity let it be said, one British officer cried, "Stop! In the name of God stop! My soul can't bear it!" But the fire of rage only did stop for the want of material. The wounded were next collected into a cart, rolled down the hill among rocks and stumps, I believe for the amusement of the soldiers. Although many will not agree with me in this, they believe the intention was to carry the wounded safely, but the steepness of the hill being such they could not control it, and so in order to save their lives were forced to let it go. Be this as it may, Sir Henry Clinton thus endorses the massacre: "The assault of Fort Griswold will impress the enemy with every apprehension of the ardor of British troops, and will hereafter be remembered with the greatest honor to the Fortieth and Forty-fourth regiments. Major Bromfield was promoted for his conduct." So the massacre was indorsed by the general, by the ministers and by the king. The plea had been offered that the laws of war allowed military executions of this sort upon a fort which persisted in a hopeless defence; but this point of the laws of war has probably never been so strained before as in this case, and in every event the wounded have been exempt. It has also been said in extenuation, that it was the outgrowth of the treatment the Tories received from the Loyalists. But who was the author of these stories of hard treatment? Rev. Samuel Peters, a Tory clergyman. But this man is also author of the statement that "the waters of the Connecticut River run so swift at Bellows Falls that an iron crowbar cannot be forced into them, but floats on the surface;" that "the inhabitants of Windham, alarmed at the noise of an invading army, kept watch all night and found in the morning a flying column of frogs on the way to the water," and a mass of other lies the devil himself would be proud to father.

As Arnold passed out of New London, the revolutionary struggle in this state passed with him, and the impression made upon the whole army was that hereafter no quarter was to be given by the British. This so fired the heart of every man in the army that with Patrick Henry he said, "Give me liberty or give me death," and with this spirit they marched on to Yorktown. The result of that march and the spirit of those men compelled Lord Cornwallis, forty-three days afterwards, to lay down his arms at the feet of General Washington. And thus it was, as Gen. Sherman said at our Centennial, "The battle of Groton Heights gave us Yorktown." With the surrender of Yorktown the British lost all hope of conquering America.

But two years more must pass before England would recognize her as a free and independent nation. And so, in order to establish the Declaration of Independence and to secure to mankind a government of the people and for the people, the only government of the kind ever known to the world, seven years of untold sufferings and hardships were absolutely necessary.

I now turn from the great act to the actors, and here one is sometimes perplexed to know whom to place at the head. It was John Adams who, on the 15th of June, 1775, nominated George Washington to command all the continental forces raised and to be raised for the defence of American liberty. It was upon that nomination the father of his country was unanimously elected. It has, I know, been said that great events make great men, but in this case I think it can be said that great men were created for the times, and the events simply called forth that which had been lying dormant. For if ever in the history of a nation a council of great men assembled, it was the first congress of this nation, Washington, Adams, Jefferson, Hancock, Franklin, and others I might name. Athens, Rome, Sparta had their great men. Some gained their distinctions by war, some by letters, others by mere chance, but it would be waste of time for me to prove that the spirit which prompted Washington and his copatriots were of that nature. In them I see an active intellect associated with extraordinary moral susceptibilities, exerting the will to its utmost daring flights, and sustaining it under its severest trials, imparting energy, zeal, vigor and life to the whole moral man. As leaders, in my humble judgment, they stand unrivalled in history. To lead in the establishment of a new order of things, in which a perfect unity of design shall be evident amidst a vast complexity of arrangements, to define with accuracy and perspicuity the reciprocal relations of rights and duties in and between individuals and societies ; to adjust the different powers and orders of a new system with such skill that every component part shall possess a peculiar orbit of action, in which the most desirable freedom may be exercised without danger of infringing upon any other portion, so as to almost preclude the possibility of mistake ; to provide for the wants and necessities of all classes of citizens of all countries, times, places and circumstances, and to breathe into the whole the breath of life, and stamp it with the impress of immobility, is a work which demands the resources of grand intellects, surpassing far that of a Solon, a Lycurgus and a Numa.

The vitality which these geniuses imparted to the system is a living demonstration of their superior intellect. Every day exhibits fresh accumulating evidence of that vitality. It grows with the growth of our country and strengthens with our strength. The century past has not written a wrinkle upon it. But to obtain it, oh ! how much precious blood had to be shed. Ledyard and Avery, Babcock and Bailey and a host of others must "jeopard their lives unto the death in the high places of the field." An attempt to analyze the characters of the Christian hero and his followers who fell in this fort would require more time than I have at command. But from what I have learned through different sources, and his own words, already quoted, as he stepped on board the boat at Fort Trumbull to cross the river for this fort, "If I must to-day lose honor or life you who know me well can tell which it will be," I believe him to have been a man that did not know how to cease doing and suffering for what he believed and knew to be right. Prompted by no mean or sordid purpose, he united with all the generosity of his nature a will that was ready and prompt, that decided while others were debating, and acted while others were deciding, driven by no fears of intimidation in the pursuit of that which he had adopted; and with all the effectiveness of purpose was a woman's gentleness. Heroic elements were in his character. For in his generous qualities were united a strong Christian faith, and the present generation loves to point to him as one of the most heroic characters of the heroic age of American history. Time fails me to dwell on the host of hero martyrs who were brutally butchered. But if ever the words of David could be appropriately applied to any people they can be here: "The beauty of Israel (God's chosen) slain upon thy high places." I venture to say, in the long history of the world, there never fell a people to whom a monument was more appropriate, than the one that stands pointing heavenward on these heights, "Where once the embattled farmers stood, and fired the shot heard round the world." And my prayer is that as long as mortar will hold stones together, this monument may stand proclaiming to future generations the wrongs of those who suffered, and the valor and glory of those who fell.

O, how that day clings to the memory! Why it is the sign and the symbol of the strife and valor and victory, as I have said, which followed at Yorktown. As high as Bunker Hill rises this tower of memory, and fitting it is that inlaid as you enter, is the marble tablet bearing the names of the fallen heroes. And future generations as they ascend its heights or gaze within, must learn the lesson of true patriotism. There are no influences more subtle, more lasting than those which proceed from the monuments of valor, worth and self-sacrifice, and the nation that does not thus keep, its youth at school to patriotism, courage and public duty, and the knowledge and praise of heroic goodness, must not expect to rear generations that shall maintain what their noble predecessors have won for them.

But Fort Griswold monument celebrates a peculiar and altogether an exalted kind of worth. Over one-half of those who fell, according to a statement made by the granddaughter of the pastor of the Congregational church in this town at the time of the battle, Rev. Aaron Kinne, were members of the church of which I am to-day his successor and pastor, and I should do a great injustice if I did not speak of my predecessor, the honored chaplain of these fallen heroes.

True, he did not fall with the many of his church, to breathe his life away weltering in his gore. For many years afterward we find him the devoted and beloved pastor of this people. A scholar of no mean order. Devoted to duty, despising hardships, he did far more than most of us would care to undertake to-day. Think of him during the great conflict in which he could have been seen carrying his flag of truce, going where duty called, administering not only to the spiritual wants of his people, but binding up their wounds. Think of his visits from house to house, and in nearly, if not all, finding it far worse than when the angel of the Lord passed over Egypt ; for not only the eldest but all the support had been slain. Wives and mothers weeping for their lost ones, and would not be comforted because they were not. Tongue cannot tell nor pencil paint the anguish of those times. Never did a minister called of God more faithfully discharge the duties of his office. And long may the acts of this true servant of God live fresh and green in the memory of this people.

And now let us guard well our sublime and holy trust, purchased at so great a price. Should the unrighteous hand of political ambition ever for a day succeed in removing our ark of civil and religious freedom, may worse than Assyrian calamities afflict the plunderers till our heavenly treasure be restored. Should human liberty ever be driven from our shores, may she find like Noah's dove no rest for the sole of her foot, till she return and find a glad people ready to receive her and love her. Let each one as an American, a man and a Christian be true to himself, that is to his knowledge and his privileges. He who is thus true to himself will be true to his fellow man, his country and his God.

Rose Hawthorne Lathrop.

The National air by the Third Regiment Band was the next number on the programme. When the echo of the music had died away Mr. Stark came to the front again to announce the poem by Mrs. Rose Hawthorne Lathrop. "Valor and patriotism in every age—in every clime—have been the inspiring theme of the poetic muse. To grace the present occasion one of the fair daughters of New England has woven a garland of poesy to decorate the fame of our heroes. The poetic tribute by Mrs. Rose Hawthorne Lathrop will now be offered by her husband, Mr. George Parsons Lathrop."

The poem, read by Mr. Lathrop, is given below. Its sentiment rose to the height of the occasion and its impressive delivery was listened to by those within hearing with unusually close attention.

THE POETIC TRIBUTE BY MRS. LATHROP.

What if upon our fortune should be sprung
A day of war?
Would not a stirring sound be flung
Of martial summons in a gush—
Keen brazen blare and drumroll's rush—
Upon the air's salt breath?
But not with joy of music they were drawn,
Whose sorrow we remember to their death.

As in a garden, with the winter near,
Another flower
And yet another gives us cheer,
Strong, fresh, unflinching in the frost;—
So,—after all the year had cost
In men,—who doubts that still
The flower of manhood rallied here, to die,
Or triumph in the mercy of God's will?

When on the harbor rose the early sails
(A pallid host
Bringing a dastard), ghostly veils
Swept from the sea, in hushing flow,
A spiritual sigh. Did nature know
The end? Soft mist delayed
The hostile fleet, which hovered, gently dim:
Yet from this vision burst the savage raid.

If in an honest cause a traitor leads,
His faithless code
Spreads murder, where the valorous deeds
Of war were just. There was a man,
Soon shackled with the whole world's ban,
Whom England found that day
To point his fellow countrymen to their graves.
From this dark name all honor turns away !

Down by the woodside there, a grave is set,
Silent, severe :
Ledyard's. And on that ground are met
The life that courage gives, the gain—
Won by the fallen, mangled, slain—
From woe how sharp, how long
We may not gauge who never felt the sword,
Up to whose hilt *his* breast endured the wrong.

About this fort,—that held a hundred men
Who drew not back,—
There flashed like silver, now and again,
From the safe, foliaged hills the guns
Of neighbors who (so history runs)
Declared themselves to stand
Ready to fight, and save their cherished lives ;
But not to *die* for their young native land.

And near this fort, guarded by dauntless men
Looking at bay
The close-swarmed enemy in the glen ;—
Those who were craftier hurried away
Their household goods and gains all day :
Up the bright river fled
Lithe ships with luxuries laden for the morrow.
But in this fort, heroes their hearts' blood shed.

For in this fort America was loved.
It seemed disgrace
To clutch at reasons to be moved
By less than their land's hope, or pride
Of manhood laboring at God's side.
What comes to men who choose
Generous right ? Alas, all story tells
These lose the most. Right, only, does not lose.

Quick aim, fierce shot ; the fort has wielded death !
A madness sprang
From the besiegers.   Hark, what saith
That dying soul there by the gate,
Who wallows in his British hate,
And craves blood for his thirst?
" Put every man to death ! "   With such a cry
Montgomery died, by his own lips accurst.

The bell of carnage was knolled forth by him !
Assassins now
Instead of soldiers, leaped the rim
Of the defended ramparts.   Where
Our troop stood firmly, thrilled the glare
From their foes' deadly eyes....
Shrewdly withdrawn, observing from afar,
Arnold's fell gaze followed his new allies.

Red as a poppy-field in slumb'rous bloom
This place became.
Hear the swift hurrying of that doom
Which in a moment lashed the forms
Of patriots, like the senseless storms
Our shores have seen, black-blown,
Instantly lifting up the measured waves
Into a turmoil with white fury strown !

Sad in defeat, but fearless, frank and cool,
Ledyard advanced :
And, with the inexorable rule
Of vanquished battle in accord,
Gave up his honorable sword
To its first touch of shame—
Shame at the hand of him who took it now,
But never dared his wretched part to claim.

As lightning falls, the sword sank in that breast
That loved the blade ;
Dashed like a serpent's fang in quest
Of the life's core which proudly made
Ledyard a man.   When he was laid,
Dead with his smile in death,
Upon that spot so many eyes have sought,
Who doubts that upward rose his smiling wraith ?

Above the moil of life, in this clear air
Where salt winds play,
Where round us gleam the wide views fair
With blue and silver of the sea,
A massacre there was to be
Such as harsh fate has hurled
When plague strides onward, meeting groups of souls
With force that strikes them low, dead to this world.

A plague kills once! These murderers struck again
For twenty times
The sinking bodies of our men,
Who,—thus surprised by sudden blight
Of devil's malice when the fight
Had closed by law of war,—
Bathed this broad mound with blood, and quenched
    the spark
Of powder till its flame could live no more.

Dead was the father, brave to bring his child
To fight for us:
Dead was the boy who in the wild
Havoc, could answer, " Never fear!"
Dead, dead and dying many, dear
As dearest ones who come,
Today, to lend their pity to the woe
Which found upon this hilltop lasting home.

Not all were dead, not every note had wailed
Its burden drear
In the funereal chant that hailed
This dark-wreathed sacrificial hour,
When misery smote with varied power
The chords of agonies deep.
Across the river's wide and shivering breast,
Heard ghostly shrill and cold, the echoes creep

Of those grim shrieks the world may seldom hear
Of bravery;
As bounding down the hill-slope sheer
The ammunition wagon goes,
Heaped with our wounded in the throes
Of bodies pierced and torn.
I hear the echo of that echo now;
And it shall sound for ages yet to mourn.

Hope was not dead.   The morning's rising sheen
Lit up the brows
Of women, trembling o'er the scene
With stern devotion, as they found
Strange shapes in writhing clusters wound,
And faces they knew not,
Although the faces were their loved ones' own.
Then hope was dead, and happiness was forgot.

If love we give, and if our tears should flow
Upon this earth
Where England dealt her cruel blow,
Still, to defeat we need not kneel.
Our radiant flag the dust might feel ;—
Yet, when disaster came,
Who won the day?   The men who slaughtered men,
Or those who, dying, have been crowned by fame?

The reading of Mrs. Lathrop's "patriotic garland of poesy" brought the exercises near the end of the programme. The anthem, "America," was sung by members of the Groton choir, the band and audience swelling out the melody so pleasingly that the hum of conversation ceased and those who did not sing were compelled to listen. "Auld Lang Syne" by the Third Regiment Band, and the benediction by Rev. W. L. Peck, completed the exercises from the platform.

THE ROUTE TO THE FERRY.

When the exercises were over the battery of regulars from Fort Trumbull fired three volleys, the sharp reports awakening the echoes of the Groton hills and reverberating to the Sound. Then the line was again formed within the fort in the order in which it was entered and the companies were ordered to proceed on the return march. The route to the ferry was through Cottage street so as to bring the procession alongside and within view of the ancient cemetery in which the body of Colonel Ledyard was interred.

On arrival at Morgan's wharf the military proceeded on board the steamer Munnatawket, which the executive committee provided for transportation to New London and thus left the ferryboat free to accommodate the public. The companies were landed at the Munnatawket's wharf, in this city, for the purpose of making a short parade.

In the order in which the procession proceeded to Fort Griswold, with the Third Regiment Band leading, the route was up State to Broad, through Broad to Hempstead, to Bulkeley place, to Richards, thus passing the old burying ground from which Benedict Arnold is said to have stood and watched the landing of the British troops and the subsequent events across the river as far as they came within his vision.

Passing through Bulkeley square the route was through Huntington to State, where the parade was reviewed from the Court-house steps by the naval officers who had been in carriages and the civic authorities.

On State street, near Bank, the soldiers from Fort Trumbull drew up in line and presented arms while the naval battalion passed with arms aport to the boats in waiting to transport them back to their respective ships.

The commemorative exercises were carefully planned, and considering the disadvantages of a forced postponement, successfully carried out from beginning to end with credit to all who participated. The kindness of Admiral Gherardi in furnishing the marine battalion and the co-operation of the commandant of Fort Trumbull, added materially to the success of the event. Aside from the centennial observance the programme of yesterday was far superior in every respect to any that preceded, not excepting that of 1826 when the corner stone of the monument was laid.

www.ingramcontent.com/pod-product-compliance
Lightning Source LLC
Chambersburg PA
CBHW030913260626
47169CB00008B/2834